Cathy J Schmidt

Illustrated by: Landon Schmidt

Tellwell Talent
www.tellwell.ca

ISBN
978-0-2288-2770-2 (Hardcover)
978-0-2288-2769-6 (Paperback)
978-0-2288-2771-9 (eBook)

Firstly, I dedicate this book to my dad, who has left us to go to Heaven. He was my supporter for so many years, and I wish I could tell him about this book.

Secondly, I owe a lot to my mom, who gave me a wonderful childhood and still does so much for me. She listens patiently to all my ramblings.

Thirdly, I want to give a big thank you to my brother, sister, and brother-in-law for their encouragement, my nephews for loving their Auntie Cat, and all the students who have come through my classroom doors for inspiring me.

–Cathy Schmidt

These illustrations are dedicated in loving memory of my dear brother Anthony.

- My childhood role model
- Far superior fisherman
- Consumer of vast quantities of caffeine
- Man I never won an argument with

But most of all, my BEST FRIEND.

Loved so much and taken too soon. Never to be forgotten.

–Landon Schmidt

Mama Mouse had four little mice. Their names were Samantha, Nicky, Tiny, and Baby. Mama Mouse loved them all very dearly. And each of these four mice said they loved their mama very much. But Mama Mouse sometimes wondered if they really did love her.

Samantha Mouse was a happy-go-lucky mouse with a carefree spirit. She loved to make big messes, but she did NOT like to clean them up! It was no fun to put away all the dolls and building blocks she liked to play with every day, and she definitely disliked making her bed. After all, it was Mama's job to do THAT!

Nicky Mouse was all boy! He loved to play outside with his tractors and make big mudholes. Mama Mouse was always reminding him to take off his dirty clothes and leave them in the mudroom.

Did Nicky Mouse ever remember to do that?

"I'm sorry, Mama," Nicky Mouse would say. "I'll remember next time!"

Mama Mouse would just heave a big sigh. She knew he would not remember next time.

Tiny Mouse was as quiet as a mouse. (Oh right, she WAS a mouse!) She loved to play with toys just like her brother and sister.

Mama Mouse was always telling Tiny and her siblings, "Put away whatever you're playing with before you play with something else."

Tiny listened to her mama and always tried really hard to clean up after herself.

Baby Mouse was just what his name says. He was a baby mouse, too little to take care of himself. Most of the time Baby Mouse was happy, kicking, and cooing all day. He loved his brother and sisters and always giggled when he watched them play.

TOYS

One dreary, rainy day, Mama Mouse was not having a good day. She tried making breadcrumbs in the morning, but the oven was too hot. She burned them.

Baby Mouse was teething. He was getting those big, big front teeth that mice are known for. It was painful for such a little guy, so he was a little fussy. Well, Mama Mouse thought he was a LOT fussy.

Nicky Mouse kept going in and out of the door of their little field house. He slammed it so hard each time, Mama Mouse was sure the back door was now the current front door. Mama Mouse's head throbbed from the noise of it all.

Samantha Mouse added to Mama Mouse's headache. Samantha was not being happy-go-lucky today. In fact, she was the absolute opposite!

Because Samantha Mouse was so grumpy, Mama Mouse was sure she had gotten up on the wrong side of the bed that morning.

But Samantha Mouse said, "I didn't get up on the wrong side. I have only one side to get up on. The other side is by the wall."

Mama Mouse sighed.

Mama Mouse headed to the kitchen to get some lunch on the table for the children. She held Baby Mouse with one arm and tried to fix lunch with her other arm.

Then Mama Mouse felt something soft brush her arm that held Baby Mouse. She looked down to see Tiny Mouse standing there, holding out her arms to take the baby.

Mama Mouse smiled tiredly. "Thank you, Tiny. You are being a big help to me today."

Tiny tickled Baby Mouse's tummy. "I can hold him for a while. I know Baby is not happy today, and I have to stay inside because of the rain."

Tiny played with Baby Mouse while Mama Mouse finished making lunch.

Nicky came running into the house, dripping rainwater all over the kitchen floor. "Just guess what I found outside, Mama?" he said in his OUTSIDE voice.

"Nicky, we don't need the groundhogs next door to hear you!" Mama Mouse quietly reminded him. "They will think we have no manners in our house."

"Oops! Sorry, Mama, but don't you want to know what I found?" Nicky held up a dripping-wet, people toothbrush. Big drops of mud fell to the floor.

"Eeewww!" squeaked Samantha. "That is so dirty!"

Nicky started chasing Samantha around the kitchen with the dirty toothbrush. She ran around the table squeaking in a shrill voice.

Just when Mama Mouse was sure it could not get any worse …

Baby Mouse started squeaking as loudly as his mousey lungs would let him. Tiny bounced Baby, but he would not stop squeaking. Mama Mouse came and took him from Tiny.

Mama Mouse stood stock still in Samantha's path and said in the sternest Mama Mouse voice she could find, "Children, you need to be quiet as mice."

(They are mice!)

"Now both of you sit down on the couch, and not a word out of you until we eat lunch."

Samantha and Nicky sat quietly until lunchtime. When Mama Mouse called them to the table, they all ran to their places. By the time they had eaten their lunch, the sun was out, so Nicky and Samantha ran outside. Mama Mouse and Tiny cleaned up the lunch mess.

Baby Mouse began to fuss again. Tiny picked him up and went to the rocking chair. She quietly rocked him to sleep and laid him down in the crib. Then she swept the floor for Mama. When she finished, she headed outside to join the others.

The little mice played together outside for most of the afternoon. Neighborhood mice came to join them in their game of hide-and-seek. All was going well until Nicky jerked Samantha's tail.

Samantha was immediately upset. Actually, she was more than upset. She turned around and the chase was on. You would have thought a cat was after Nicky with how fast he was running.

"Run, Nicky, run!" the boy mice called out to him.

"Run, Samantha, run!" the girl mice called out to her.

Nicky was sure he was going to get away from Samantha, but just as he rounded the corner of their little field house …

There stood Tiny. She was not looking so tiny at the moment. She had her paws on her hips and her feet were braced to stop Nicky in his flight.

"Stop and listen!" Tiny told both her brother and sister. "Mama is having a bad day, and we should make it easier for her. I have an idea of what we can do to help."

Nicky and Samantha looked at each other.

"I'm sorry I pulled your tail, Samantha," said Nicky with a small smile.

Samantha hugged him. "That's okay, but don't let it happen again." She gave Nicky a smile.

"Good for you both! Now here is my idea ..." Tiny excitedly told them how she thought they could help Mama Mouse.

Nicky, Samantha, and Tiny went sneaking into the house. They did not want Mama Mouse to see them. They peeked into the kitchen, but Mama Mouse was not in there.

They hurried through the kitchen and peeked around the corner into the living room. They saw Mama Mouse was holding Baby Mouse in the rocking chair. Mama and Baby were both sound asleep.

Nicky, Samantha, and Tiny tiptoed through the living room, being as quiet as mice, of course. Finally, they made it to the bedrooms.

Samantha saw her unmade bed. She scampered to the bed to start making it. She felt a warm feeling come over her. It felt good to help Mama.

Nicky saw the blocks they had left out from earlier in the day. He knelt on the floor, picked up all the blocks, and put the container away.

As he put the container on the shelf, he wondered, "Why does my heart feel warm and fuzzy? It must be because I helped Mama."

Nicky took off with a smile, searching for another way to help.

Tiny picked Baby's blanket up off the floor. She also straightened up the game closet in the hallway. She felt so happy, and she knew it was because they were helping Mama.

The three happy (not blind!) mice met up in the hallway. In quiet voices, they decided to go to the kitchen to make one more surprise for Mama. They stifled their happy giggles and went sneaking into the kitchen. They glanced into the living room and saw that Mama was still sleeping.

They all let out a big sigh of relief when they made it back to the kitchen. The girls started washing the dishes left over from lunch. It was so hard to be quiet as mice at a time like this! Nicky started to set the table for supper. They were so busy trying to be quiet that they did not hear Mama come into the kitchen.

"What's going on?" Mama Mouse asked.

Her happy voice made them all jump with surprise.

"It looks like my little mice are being such BIG helpers today. It makes me feel even more warm and fuzzy than I already do being a mouse. Come here, my dears, so I can give you all a kiss!"

The girls quickly scampered to get their reward from Mama, but Nicky got a horrified look on his face, and his whiskers twitched something awful. Mama Mouse kissed the girls with a big smack and quietly sneaked up on Nicky. She grabbed him and gave him a big mousey squeeze.

That evening, when the family was sitting around the supper table, they were all smiling. Even Baby was smiling and showing off the new white nubs that were starting to show in his mouth.

Daddy Mouse looked proud of his brood, and Mama Mouse was exclaiming about how helpful her dear little mice had been.

"It makes this daddy really happy to know his little ones are learning to be so helpful. Keep up the good work," Daddy said, smiling at them all.

Later, as Mama Mouse was tucking her little mice into bed, she leaned over to kiss Samantha. Samantha's arms wrapped around her mother exuberantly. "I love you so much, Mama!"

"I love you, too, my happy Samantha," Mama whispered into her ear.

Next, Mama Mouse went to Nicky's bed to tuck his blankets around him. As she leaned over him, he whispered so the girls could NOT hear, "I love you to the moon and back, Mama."

Mama smiled at her mischievous, tough son. "I love you, too, my handsome guy." She ruffled his fur.

Tiny smiled a big smile when Mama came to her bed last. "Oh, Mama, I love you so much my heart feels like it's going to go 'Poof'," she said quietly.

Mama Mouse hugged her little girl and whispered into her ear, "I love you, too, my quiet helper."

As Mama Mouse walked through the doorway, she looked back at her little mice. She no longer wondered if they loved her. Mama Mouse smiled as she closed their bedroom door.

About the Author

Cathy loves teaching her students every day. Storytime is her favorite time of day as she tries to make the books that she reads to her students come alive. Besides reading, she likes to go camping and dreams of traveling to faraway places.

Lightning Source UK Ltd.
Milton Keynes UK
UKHW021523171220
375250UK00004B/62

9 780228 827702